MAGIC TREE HOUSE®

#36 SUNLIGHT ON THE SNOW LEOPARD

Dear Reader,

Did you know there's a Magic Tree House® book for every kid? From those just starting to read chapter books to more experienced readers, Magic Tree House® has something for everyone, including science, sports, geography, wildlife, history... and always a bit of mystery and magic!

Magic Tree House®
Adventures with Jack and Annie, perfect for readers who are just starting to read chapter books.
F&P Level: M

**Magic Tree House®
Merlin Missions**
More challenging adventures for the experienced Magic Tree House® reader.
F&P Levels: M–N

**Magic Tree House®
Super Edition**
A longer and more dangerous adventure with Jack and Annie.
F&P Level: P

**Magic Tree House®
Fact Trackers**
Nonfiction companions to your favorite Magic Tree House® adventures.
F&P Levels: N–X

Happy reading!

Mary Pope Osborne

... IC
TREE HOUSE®

#36 SUNLIGHT ON THE SNOW LEOPARD

BY MARY POPE OSBORNE

ILLUSTRATED BY AG FORD

A STEPPING STONE BOOK™

Random House ⌂ New York

Visit us on the Web!
rhcbooks.com
MagicTreeHouse.com

Educators and librarians, for a variety of teaching tools,
visit us at RHTeachersLibrarians.com

Library of Congress Cataloging-in-Publication Data
Names: Osborne, Mary Pope, author. | Ford, AG, illustrator. | Magic tree house series.
Title: Sunlight on the snow leopard / by Mary Pope Osborne; illustrated by AG Ford.
Description: New York: Random House, [2022] | Series: Magic tree house | "A Stepping Stone book." | Summary: The magic tree house is back with a message from Morgan le Fay telling Jack and Annie to seek out the Gray Ghost and listen to her story, and immediately they are whisked away to Nepal where they meet Tenzin, a climber who has recently lost his family, and who takes them up the mountain to meet a snow leopard and renew himself.
Identifiers: LCCN 2021013214 (print) | LCCN 2021013215 (ebook) |
ISBN 978-0-593-17750-1 (hardcover) | ISBN 978-0-593-17751-8 (library binding) |
ISBN 978-0-593-17752-5 (ebook)
Subjects: LCSH: Annie (Fictitious character from Osborne)—Juvenile fiction. | Jack (Fictitious character from Osborne)—Juvenile fiction. | Snow leopard—Juvenile fiction. | Magic—Juvenile fiction. | Sherpa (Nepalese people)—Juvenile fiction. | Quests (Expeditions)—Juvenile fiction. | Bereavement—Juvenile fiction. | Tree houses—Juvenile fiction. | Nepal—Juvenile fiction. | CYAC: Space and time—Fiction. | Magic—Fiction. | Snow leopard—Fiction. | Leopard—Fiction. | Characters in literature—Fiction. | Sherpa (Nepalese people)—Fiction. | Grief—Fiction. | Nepal—Fiction.
Classification: LCC PZ7.O81167 Stp 2022 (print) | LCC PZ7.O81167 (ebook) |
DDC 813.54 [Fic]—dc23

Printed in the United States of America
10 9 8 7 6 5 4 3 2 1

This book has been officially leveled by using the F&P Text Level Gradient™ Leveling System.

For Gerard "GG" Garvey

 CONTENTS

PROLOGUE

One summer day in Frog Creek, Pennsylvania, a mysterious tree house appeared in the woods. It was filled with books. A boy named Jack and his sister, Annie, found the tree house and soon discovered that it was magic. They could go to any time and place in history just by pointing to a picture in one of the books. While they were gone, no time at all passed back in Frog Creek.

Jack and Annie eventually found out that the tree house belonged to Morgan le Fay, a magical librarian from the legendary realm of Camelot.

Since then, they have traveled on many adventures in the magic tree house and completed many missions for Morgan.

On their most recent adventures, Jack and Annie have spent time with some extraordinary creatures around the world: a narwhal, a llama, and a grizzly bear. Now they are about to set out once more to explore the wondrous world of nature.

1
A Rainy Day

The late-winter air was wet and chilly. Rain was falling.

Jack sat on the front porch. He was taking notes on a book about grizzly bears.

"There you are!" said Annie, standing in the doorway.

"Yep. Here I am," said Jack, still writing.

"It's raining," said Annie.

"Yep," Jack said.

"Day after day," said Annie. "It's so dreary."

"Yep," said Jack.

"You want to do something?" Annie asked.

"Nope," Jack said.

"We could make mud pies," said Annie.

"Right," Jack said without looking up.

"Or help worms cross the road!" said Annie.

"Good one," said Jack.

"Study raindrops through our microscope?" said Annie.

"Hey, I think I hear Mom calling you," said Jack.

"Very funny," said Annie.

"No, really," said Jack. He covered his mouth and faked their mom's voice. "An-nie!"

Annie laughed. She stepped out onto the porch and looked at the falling rain. "Whoa," she said after a moment. "I think I really did hear something. It wasn't Mom. And it wasn't you."

Jack looked up. "You're kidding, right?" he said.

"Nope! Not kidding," said Annie. "It's calling us!"

"Oh, man. You were right the last time that happened," said Jack. He closed his notebook and stood up. "Okay. You win."

"Yay!" said Annie. She disappeared inside the house. "Mom, Dad! Jack and I are going for a walk!"

"Okay. But be back in twenty minutes for an early dinner!" their mom called.

"You'll need raincoats and boots!" their dad shouted.

A moment later Annie came back with two pairs of rubber boots and two slick yellow raincoats. She and Jack pulled them on.

Jack put his notebook and pencil in his pocket. He and Annie left the porch and ran across their soggy yard. They started up the sidewalk, splashing through big puddles. Cars swished past them in the rain.

Soon Jack and Annie crossed the street and headed into the Frog Creek woods. Their boots squished over the wet ground.

They made their way between the bare trees until they came to the tallest oak.

"Yay! I heard right!" Annie said.

"Yep! You did!" said Jack.

The magic tree house *was* back. It was tucked into the highest branches.

Annie grabbed the rope ladder and started up. Jack followed her.

The tree house was damp inside. A small book was lying in the corner. Annie grabbed it.

"It's a tourist guide!" she said.

"Cool, so where are we going?" asked Jack. "I hope it's warm and sunny."

"Forget it," said Annie. She held up the book. The cover showed snow-covered mountains. The title was:

HIKING IN NEPAL

7

Darn, thought Jack. He was tired of cold rain and snow.

"Nepal? Where's that?" said Annie.

"I'm not sure," said Jack. "But I know it's where the Himalayas are, including Mount Everest. That's the highest peak in the world."

Annie opened the guide book. There was a map on the inside cover. "There!" she said. She pointed to the small country of Nepal, tucked between India and China.

"We've been to that part of the world," said Jack.

"I know!" said Annie. "Remember the silk weaver in China? And riding elephants in India? Now we can add *hiking in Nepal* to the list."

"Right," said Jack. "Is there a note in the book?"

Annie shook the guide book. A folded slip of paper fell out.

"Thank you, Morgan!" Annie said. She picked up the paper and read a message from Morgan le Fay:

Dear Jack and Annie,

The Gray Ghost of the Mountains,
The phantom of snow,
Has a secret to tell you
That very few know.

Alone on the hillside,
She hides in plain sight.

Her wisdom speaks softly
In shadows and light.

Ask those around you
Where the ghost can be found.
Follow the one
Who says "higher ground."

Let your hearts be open
And your minds be free.
Write down her secret
And share it with me.

"*The Gray Ghost!*" said Annie, her eyes wide.

"I wonder what that means," Jack said anxiously. "I'll check the book." He turned to the back of their Nepal guide. "Nope. No *Gray Ghost* in the index."

Annie looked back at the rhyme. "Maybe that's why Morgan says, '*Ask those around you*

10

where the ghost can be found.' That sounds easy enough."

"I guess . . . ," said Jack.

"Ready to go?" said Annie.

"Yeah . . . sure," said Jack, shivering. Hiking in cold gray weather didn't sound fun at all. Plus, he was actually a little afraid of ghosts.

"Are you nervous about something?" said Annie.

"No, I'm fine," said Jack.

"Don't worry," said Annie. "The Gray Ghost is probably just part of a legend or a story."

Jack felt a little better. "Okay. Let's go for it." He pointed to the cover of the Nepal guide. "I wish we could go there!" he said.

The wind started to blow.

The tree house started to spin.

It spun faster and faster.

Then everything was still.

Absolutely still.

2

WE SALUTE YOU!

The air in Nepal was cold and dry.

"Wow, our clothes look like they came from our time," said Annie.

"Right," said Jack.

Annie and Jack wore parkas with hoods, gloves, wool pants and hats, and hiking boots. Jack's notebook was in a pocket of his parka. Two large red backpacks were on the floor.

"Wow! These are nice packs!" said Annie. "I wonder what's in them."

"Yeah, why are they so big?" asked Jack.

Jack and Annie each unzipped a backpack and looked inside.

"A rolled-up sleeping bag!" said Jack.

"Cool," said Annie. "We can sleep anywhere we want."

"So, where are we?" said Jack.

He and Annie looked out the tree house window.

They'd landed in a small hemlock grove. Beyond the woods, everything looked dreary: a brown, wintry pasture; lonely stone huts; and treeless gray mountains.

"It's gloomy here, too," said Jack.

"You can say that again," said Annie.

"It's gloomy here, too," said Jack.

Jack and Annie leaned out the window. Beyond the hemlocks was a stream. Two young girls in red dresses were kneeling on the bank.

Both had flowing, dark hair and were talking and laughing while they worked. They were scrubbing a pile of wooden plates and bowls.

"We can ask *them* about the Gray Ghost," said Annie. "Come on! Let's go down."

"It's a start," said Jack.

Annie slipped Morgan's rhyme into a pocket of her parka. Jack put their guide book into his backpack.

Then they climbed down the rope ladder.

Jack and Annie walked out from the hemlock grove and headed to the stream bank.

When the girls caught sight of them, they cried out with excitement. They put the bowls aside and jumped to their feet.

Each girl pressed her hands together and bowed her head. "I salute you!" they called out together.

Annie copied the girls. She put her hands together, too, and bowed her head.

"*We* salute *you!*" she said. "I'm Annie. He's my brother, Jack."

"I'm Mina!" said the older girl. "She's my sister, Fuli."

The younger girl gave them a big grin. She was missing her two front teeth.

"Are you travelers?" asked Mina.

"Yes!" said Annie. "We're hikers, actually."

"Did you come to our village for the festival?" asked Mina.

"No . . . we're just hiking," said Jack.

"We came from America," said Annie. "We're looking for something called the Gray Ghost of the Mountains. Have you heard of her?"

"No, I haven't," said Mina.

"They should ask Tenzin!" Fuli said.

"Who's that?" said Annie.

"Tenzin is the storyteller in our village," said Mina. "He knows all the stories about the mountains."

"He was once a mountain guide!" said Fuli.

"Yes, Tenzin used to lead climbers," said Mina. "He carried their gear, made their tea. But he no longer does that."

"He doesn't do anything now," said Fuli in a sad voice.

"Why?" said Annie.

"Because he's too sad. He was left all alone," said Fuli.

Jack wondered what that meant.

"He might know a story about a gray ghost, though," said Mina. "Would you like to visit him?"

"Sure," said Jack.

"We'll take you!" said Mina.

The sisters quickly packed their clean plates and bowls into two bamboo baskets. Then each girl strapped a basket on to her back.

"Follow us!" said Mina.

"Wait, can we help carry your stuff?" asked Jack.

"No, we carry heavy things every day," said Mina.

"Every day!" Fuli chimed in with a grin.

Under the cloudy late-afternoon sky, the girls led Jack and Annie down a dirt path through an open pasture. Even with their heavy baskets, they walked quickly.

Jack and Annie hurried after Mina and Fuli. They passed black cattle and gray sheep grazing in the brown winter grass.

They passed other people with heavy loads, too—children with bundles of sticks and older people with bales of hay on their backs.

Everyone seems to work really hard here, Jack thought.

But as they scurried along, the sisters were cheerful. They laughed with each other. And Fuli kept looking back and smiling her big toothless grin.

Jack and Annie followed them through tangled weeds. Then they headed up a steep path to a small hut at the edge of the village. The hut was nestled against the side of a mountain slope.

"Tenzin!" called Fuli. "Tenzin!"

"I am here," a soft voice called from the flat rooftop.

"It's Mina and Fuli!" called Mina. "We brought two visitors! Can we come up?"

Tenzin didn't answer.

"We'd better check on him," said Mina.

The sisters put down their baskets. Then they scrambled up a wooden ladder to Tenzin's rooftop.

3

TENZIN

Jack and Annie set their backpacks beside the girls' baskets. Then they climbed up the ladder to the flat roof.

Tenzin was lying on a straw mattress in the chilly open air. His eyes were closed.

"Tenzin, are you well?" asked Mina.

"Yes . . . fine . . . ," the man said. He struggled to sit up.

Jack was surprised. He thought a mountain climber would look really strong.

But Tenzin was small and thin. His face was lined with wrinkles.

Mina and Fuli put their hands together and bowed their heads. Jack and Annie did the same.

"I salute you," each of them said.

Tenzin nodded.

"This is Jack and Annie. They're hikers from America," said Mina.

Tenzin barely glanced at them.

"Annie and Jack are searching for a story about a gray ghost," said Mina.

Tenzin looked up sharply. "The Gray Ghost?" he said.

"Yes," said Annie. "Mina said you might know some stories about her."

"Do you?" said Jack.

Tenzin stared at them for a moment. "Why do you want to know about the Gray Ghost?" he asked.

"A friend wants us to find out about it," said

22

Annie. "She told us to ask people in Nepal. We thought it might be part of a mountain legend."

"We're just curious," Jack said. He didn't want Tenzin to know he was afraid of ghosts.

"Ah. Just curious," said Tenzin. He sighed. "No. I fear I cannot help you."

"Well, thank you anyway, Tenzin," said Mina.

"We have to hurry home now and help Ama. We salute you."

Mina and Fuli left the rooftop. Jack followed them down the ladder. But Annie stayed behind.

Back on the ground, Mina turned to Jack. "I invite you to come home with us, to meet our mother," she said.

"Ama takes good care of travelers!" said Fuli.

"Great. Thank you," said Jack.

"But we must hurry," said Mina. "We have to help her during the dinner hour." She and Fuli strapped their baskets on to their backs.

"Annie!" Jack called. "We have to leave!"

"Be right there!" Annie shouted from the rooftop.

They all waited. But Annie still didn't come down.

Jack sighed. "I'll get her," he said. He climbed back up the ladder.

Jack saw Annie kneeling next to Tenzin. She was holding Morgan's rhyme. She had started to read:

The Gray Ghost of the Mountains,
The phantom of snow,
Has a secret to tell you
That very few know.

Alone on the hillside,
She hides in plain sight.
Her wisdom speaks softly
In shadows and light.

Before Annie could read more, Tenzin stopped her. "Who gave you these words?" he asked.

"Our friend Morgan," said Annie. "She's a master storyteller, like you."

"And she is your friend?" said Tenzin.

"Yes," said Annie.

"It is a very wise person who wrote those words," he said. "I will help you."

"You will?" said Jack, moving closer to them. He was amazed that Annie had changed Tenzin's mind.

"Yes. But only if you are serious about your quest," Tenzin said to Jack. "Not merely curious."

"We're serious. *Very* serious," said Jack.

"Actually, looking for the Gray Ghost is our whole reason for being here," said Annie.

"I see. Well, perhaps we can learn her secret together," he said. "Come back at first light."

"Oh, wow! Thanks!" said Annie.

"Yes, thanks! See you then!" said Jack.

He and Annie climbed down the ladder.

"Did you learn anything more from Tenzin?" Mina asked.

Jack and Annie strapped on their backpacks.

"We shared our friend's letter with him," said Annie. "And he told us he would help us!"

"Tomorrow, at first light," said Jack.

"Good," said Mina. "But now we should hurry home."

"This way!" said Fuli.

In the growing dark, they all walked down the steep path. They waded through the tall grasses.

Chickens scattered out of their way as they hurried past a row of stone huts. Woodsmoke rose into the sky.

"We live *there!*" Fuli called out. She pointed to a hut that was more colorful than the rest. It had a red roof and a blue wooden door.

A sign in a window read:

AMA'S TEA HOUSE

"Welcome, Jack and Annie!" said Mina.

A string of brass bells jingled as she pushed open the blue door.

4

AMA'S TEA HOUSE

Ama's Tea House was smoky and dimly lit. A woodstove and several oil lanterns cast a cozy light over the room.

Mina and Fuli placed their baskets inside the door. Jack and Annie dropped their backpacks there, too. They hung their parkas on hooks on the wall.

A woman in a long brown apron came out from the kitchen.

"Ama! We brought new friends home!" Fuli called out. "Jack and Annie!"

28

The woman smiled. Her black hair gleamed in the firelight.

"Welcome, new friends!" she said.

Annie pressed her hands together. "We salute you, Ama," she said.

Ama laughed warmly. "And I salute you. Who are you? Where are you from?"

"We're Jack and Annie," said Annie.

"A brother and sister from America!" said Fuli.

"Wonderful," said Ama. "But you are so young. Where are your parents?"

Jack cleared his throat. "Well . . . actually, we'll see them tomorrow."

"They gave us a day on our own," said Annie.

"Really?" said Ama. She shook her head. "They must trust you very much to give you such freedom. But please, allow me to take care of you before they arrive."

"Okay, sure. Thanks," said Jack.

"Sit at a table," said Ama. "And we will bring you some dinner. Come, girls. Help me."

The two sisters followed their mother back to the kitchen. Jack and Annie sat at an empty table and looked around.

Through the smoky haze, Jack saw men playing cards. They looked like they came from the village. They had weathered faces and wore long shirts and vests.

At another table sat a group of young hikers. They had large backpacks and walking sticks. They were laughing and looking at maps.

Ama and her daughters came out of the kitchen, carrying food.

"For you, Jack and Annie!" Fuli said. She put down a plate of fried bread.

Mina set down little pots of butter and honey.

Ama gave them bowls of lentil soup.

"Thanks!" said Annie.

31

Jack thought the soup smelled like a dish their mom made at home. It made him feel a little homesick.

As he and Annie started eating, Ama and the girls sat down at their table.

"So you have traveled here for the festival?" asked Ama.

"No, not really," said Annie.

What festival? Jack wondered as he spread butter and honey over a piece of bread.

Before he could ask, Fuli jumped in. "They came here to find a story about a gray ghost!" she said.

"So we took them to meet Tenzin!" said Mina. "We told them he was a great storyteller."

"Tenzin said he will help them tomorrow," said Fuli.

"Oh?" said Ama. "That's wonderful! Tenzin hardly ever sees visitors now. He's not been well. And he certainly doesn't tell stories anymore."

"Why? What's wrong?" asked Annie.

"Tenzin has a broken heart," said Fuli.

"What happened to him?" said Jack.

"His wife and daughter died of the fever last winter," said Ama. "He couldn't get them to a hospital in time. The closest one is far away." Tears came to her eyes.

Jack thought of the man living all alone in his mountain hut. Then he thought about how he would feel if he didn't have Annie or his parents.

"That's terrible," he said.

"Yes, it is," said Ama. "The whole village has missed him. Before he lost his family, he would stop by the tea house every day. He carried wood for the elderly. He taught climbing skills to the little ones. It is good that you are going to visit him tomorrow."

"I hope we can cheer him up," said Annie.

"Me too," said Ama with a smile. "Come, girls,

we must clean up now. Mina, collect payments. Fuli, clear the tables, please."

Mina and Fuli jumped up and started helping their mother.

"Poor Tenzin," Annie said to Jack.

"Yeah. Really," he said.

The other customers were starting to leave. Soon they were all gone. The lanterns were nearly out, and the fire was low. The tea room had grown chilly.

"Jack and Annie, since your parents do not arrive until tomorrow, you must stay with us tonight," said Ama.

"Thanks!" said Annie.

"The girls and I sleep in the small attic upstairs. But you and your brother can sleep in this room. We will bring you some blankets."

"That's okay, don't worry," said Jack. "We have sleeping bags in our backpacks."

"Wonderful," said Ama. "Come, girls. To bed. Tomorrow is a big day."

"The festival!" said Fuli, clapping her hands.

"Good night!" said Mina. She and her sister followed Ama up steep wooden stairs to the attic.

Jack and Annie pulled off their hiking boots. They unrolled their sleeping bags and crawled inside them.

"Ohh, this is nice," said Annie. "I feel warm and toasty."

"Me too," said Jack.

"It's so quiet and peaceful here," murmured Annie. "No cars. No trucks. No computers. No television. No radio. No phones. . . ." She yawned.

"Yeah, it is a peaceful place," said Jack. But he thought it was a sad place, too. The people worked so hard, yet they seemed poor. And there were no hospitals nearby.

"I'm wondering what that festival is," said Annie, yawning again.

"Tomorrow we'll check our guide book," said Jack.

"I feel bad about Tenzin," said Annie.

"Me too," said Jack.

"Maybe tomorrow we can . . ." Her voice trailed off.

"We can *what*?" said Jack.

Annie didn't answer. She was asleep.

Jack finished her sentence. "Maybe tomorrow we can help him . . . ," he said softly.

Then he closed his eyes. And he, too, fell fast asleep.

5

FIRST LIGHT

A rooster crowed outside.

"Wake up, Jack! It's first light!" said Annie.

Jack opened his eyes.

Light came through the windowpanes. The fire had gone out. The room was freezing.

Jack wanted to stay in his sleeping bag. But he stretched and got up with Annie. They pulled on their parkas, hiking boots, and gloves. They rolled up their sleeping bags and pulled on their backpacks.

Annie opened the blue door, and she and Jack slipped out of Ama's Tea House.

As they hurried through the gray dawn, Jack could see his breath in the cold air. Villagers were already at work.

Small children were feeding chickens. An old woman was milking a cow. Girls were herding sheep into the frosty pasture.

Jack and Annie tramped through the tall grass. They climbed the path to Tenzin's house.

To Jack's surprise, the frail-looking man was standing outside. He wore no jacket, gloves, or shoes.

"Good morning!" Tenzin said. "Are you ready to hike up that hill?" He pointed at the rocky slope rising above his hut.

The hill looked like a high mountain to Jack! "You mean hike up that mountain?" he said.

Tenzin smiled. "Some may call it a mountain," he said. "But to me, it is only a high hill."

"What's up there?" asked Annie.

"If we are blessed, we will see the Gray Ghost," said Tenzin.

"Oh, wow," whispered Annie.

"Um . . . so the Gray Ghost isn't just a character in a story?" said Jack.

"No. She is real," said Tenzin. "Very real."

"Oh . . . she's real," Jack said in a small voice.

"You okay with that?" Annie whispered to him.

He nodded and looked back at Tenzin.

"But—don't you need warmer clothes? Or at least shoes?" Jack asked.

"I have climbed all my life without shoes," said Tenzin. "I am not afraid to do so now."

"But do you feel strong enough?" said Jack.

"Yes!" said Tenzin. "The letter you read to me last evening stirred some memories. It has brought back a bit of strength."

"So . . . how far do you think we should hike?" asked Jack.

"Until the Gray Ghost sees us," said Tenzin.

"You mean until *we* see *her*?" said Annie.

"No. She can best be seen when one is *not* looking for her," Tenzin said.

How do you not look for something that you're looking for? thought Jack.

"One can even gaze right at her and fail to see her," said Tenzin.

"So, what does one do to find her?" Annie asked.

"One can only hope to be in the right place at the right time," said Tenzin.

Annie smiled. "I understand," she said.

She does? thought Jack.

"Good. Then let us begin our journey!" said Tenzin. He turned and started hiking up the rock-covered slope behind his hut.

"Ready?" Annie asked Jack.

"No. Listen—we shouldn't encourage him," said Jack. "Ama said he's not been well. He's not dressed warmly enough, and he's not making sense. We have to stop him."

"How?" said Annie.

"I don't know," said Jack. Then he shouted, "TENZIN!"

Tenzin turned around and waved at them.

"Leave your backpacks by my door!" he shouted. "Follow me to higher ground!" And he started hiking up the slope again.

"Oh, man," said Jack. "What should we do?"

"Wait, wait—did he just say *higher ground*?" said Annie. She grabbed Morgan's note from her pocket. She read aloud:

Ask those around you
Where the ghost can be found.
Follow the one
Who says "higher ground."

"Yes! Tenzin said Morgan's words!" said Annie. "He *literally* said, *Follow me to higher ground!*"

"Whoa," said Jack.

"So we *have* to follow him!" said Annie. "We don't have a choice!"

Jack took a deep breath. "You're right," he said.

He and Annie set their backpacks outside Tenzin's door. Then they started up the rocky slope, following Tenzin to higher ground.

6

YAK, NAK, AND IBEX

Tenzin was hiking quickly up the slope of the high hill. In his bare feet, he sprang from rock to rock. He leapt over dark crevices between boulders.

"He's so fast!" said Annie.

"I know!" said Jack. "We have to catch up!"

But catching up to Tenzin wasn't easy. Jack slipped on some loose rocks and nearly hit his head on a boulder.

"Jack! You okay?" said Annie.

"Sure, no problem," Jack said, jumping to his feet. "Keep going."

"Oh, wait!" said Annie. "Look!"

She pointed to a strange-looking animal walking along a ledge. It had enormous curved horns.

"What's *that*?" said Jack.

"An ibex! It's a wild mountain goat!" said Annie.

"Cool," said Jack.

More ibexes trailed out from behind large boulders.

Jack and Annie watched the mountain goats clomp down over the rocks and disappear around a lower ledge.

"Oh, look at that! It's a *yak*!" said Annie.

"A *yak*?" said Jack.

"Yes!" said Annie. She pointed to a creature standing near the base of the slope. It had horns, too, and long, dark, shaggy hair. "I've always wanted to see a yak! Did you know a female yak is called a *nak*?"

"No," said Jack, shaking his head. "You really know a lot about animals, Annie."

"Not really. I just know a little about a lot of them," she said. She turned back around. "Look at Tenzin now! He's nearly out of sight!"

"TENZIN, WAIT!" Jack shouted.

But Tenzin didn't seem to hear him.

"We have to catch up!" said Jack.

Jack and Annie kept climbing over pebbles and rocks. The hike soon became harder as the slope grew steeper.

Snow covered the higher part of the mountain. And the wind blew against them.

"Jack, stop! Look!" said Annie.

She pointed to another creature. It was small and round with bushy gray fur.

"Squirrel?" said Jack.

"Marmot!" said Annie. "Marmots are the heaviest members of the squirrel family."

"Cool," said Jack. "But we can't keep stopping, okay? We can't lose sight of Tenzin!"

"Right!" said Annie.

"We have to go faster," said Jack. He shot ahead of Annie and climbed faster.

Too fast.

Jack slipped on a snow-covered rock and fell to the ground. The rock tumbled down the slope, causing a rockslide. More rocks rolled down, heading toward Annie.

Annie jumped out of the way. But she slipped and fell, too. She scrambled on her hands and knees over the snow and hid behind a boulder. More rocks crashed down the slope.

"Annie!" cried Jack.

"I'm okay!" Annie shouted. "Are you okay?"

"Yes!" said Jack.

After a moment, the rocks stopped sliding. Annie peeked out from behind the boulder. "All clear?" she called to Jack.

"All clear!" he called back.

Annie hurried to catch up with Jack.

"Tenzin must not realize that we fell," said Annie. "I can't see him at all anymore."

"Me neither," said Jack. "Oh, man, he can't keep this up. He's got to rest soon. Maybe he's up on that ridge." Jack pointed to a narrow ledge farther up the mountainside.

"I wonder how high is *higher ground*," said Annie.

"I have no idea," said Jack. "Let's go. Watch your step."

They both started hiking again. As they drew close to the ridge, Jack shouted, "TENZIN!"

This time, he heard a call. "I'm here!"

"Whew," said Jack. He and Annie hauled themselves over the ridge and saw Tenzin.

He was sitting on a rock, waiting for them. He didn't look tired at all. He wasn't even breathing hard.

"Are . . . you . . . okay?" said Annie, panting.

"It is going well!" said Tenzin. "And how are you?"

"We're great," said Annie.

Not really, thought Jack.

"I'm thinking maybe we should hike back down now," Jack said to Tenzin. "We could go to Ama's Tea House. And you could *tell* us about the Gray Ghost."

"Forgive me," said Tenzin. "I fear I have put you and Annie at risk. Please, do return to the village."

"Without you?" said Annie.

"Yes. Without me. Now that I have begun, I must keep to my journey. We are so close," said Tenzin.

Close to what? Jack wondered. He started to protest. But Tenzin raised his hand.

"Listen!" he said.

Jack listened. He didn't hear anything. In fact, the air had become oddly still. There was no sound of wind.

"She is watching us," Tenzin whispered. "I can feel it."

Jack felt a chill run down his spine.

"Who's watching?" said Annie.

Suddenly a piercing scream came from higher up the mountain.

7

GIANT PAWS

"What was that?" Jack said, frightened.

"I must go!" said Tenzin.

"Go where?" said Jack. "Back down?"

But Tenzin leapt to his feet and started *up* the snow-covered slope again.

"Wait, Tenzin! We'll come with you!" said Annie.

"No, Annie! Stop!" said Jack.

She stopped.

"What was that scream?" Jack said.

"I don't know! Stay here, and I'll come back

and tell you!" said Annie. She hurried up the slope after Tenzin.

Jack froze. His heart was pounding. *Who screamed? The Gray Ghost?* He wanted to hurry *away* from the scream, not toward it.

Tenzin and Annie were about to climb out of sight. Jack didn't want anything bad to happen to either of them.

"I'm coming! Wait!" he shouted.

Annie waited.

Jack scrambled over the rocks and caught up with her. "We've got to go back down!" he said. "Now!"

"And leave Tenzin?" said Annie.

"No, no! We can't leave him!" said Jack. "We have to catch up to him and convince him to come with us!"

They looked up the snowy slope. "He's vanished again," said Annie. "How did he do that?"

"He's an expert climber," said Jack. "But why is he chasing that scream? What *was* it?"

"I—I'm not sure . . . the Gray Ghost?" said Annie. For once, she looked a little frightened.

Jack took a deep breath. He knew he had to be brave, for Annie and for Tenzin. "Don't worry," he said. "We just have to find Tenzin. We'll be all right. Let's go."

Jack and Annie started back up, their boots crunching over the snow. As they climbed, there was still no sign of Tenzin.

"Whoa!" Annie said.

"What?" said Jack.

She pointed at the ground. There were footprints in the snow.

"Are those animal paws?" said Jack.

"Yes," said Annie.

"They're huge!" said Jack. "What kind of animal is that?"

"Definitely some kind of a cat," Annie said.

"But a really big cat, right?" said Jack. "Like a wild tiger or a lion?"

"Not a lion—they only live in Africa," said Annie. "But a tiger . . . maybe."

Jack took a deep breath. "Whatever it is, it's really, really big."

"Big cats can be dangerous to humans," Annie said. "What if it finds Tenzin before we do?"

A part of Jack wanted to race back down the mountain. But now he was more worried for Tenzin than himself.

"We have to find him before the big cat does," he said.

"Right," said Annie. They kept hiking up the snow-covered slope.

"Look—more tracks!" Annie said. "They lead that way!"

They turned to the right.

"And more prints there!" said Jack.

"Where?" said Annie.

"Going that way!" said Jack. They kept following the tracks.

Annie came to a sudden stop. "Oh, wow!" she breathed.

Jack studied the ground for more tracks.

"I don't believe it!" Annie said in a hushed voice.

"What? More tracks?" Jack asked.

"You don't see it?" said Annie.

Jack looked all around. He didn't see anything special. Just boulders, smaller rocks, and snow.

"No. What? Where?" he asked.

"There! Tenzin!" She pointed.

"Where? Where?" he said.

"You're looking right at them!" said Annie.

"Them?" said Jack.

At that moment, something moved and growled softly.

A *very* big cat was peering at Jack and Annie.

The cat was hiding in plain sight. Its spotted white-and-gray fur blended perfectly with the white-gray mountain rocks.

The cat had a large head and big paws. It had a huge furry tail, nearly as long as its body.

The huge tail was tucked around Tenzin.

Jack nearly fainted.

"A snow leopard!" said Annie softly. "No one ever sees a snow leopard."

Leopard? Jack thought with terror. Had the leopard hurt Tenzin?

"Tenzin! Are you okay?" he said.

"Do not worry. I am safe with my friend," Tenzin called back. "You are safe, too. She is grateful to you for bringing us together again. Come forward."

Jack and Annie slowly crossed the rocks, drawing closer to the snow leopard.

The big cat didn't move. She just kept staring at Jack and Annie with her pale-green eyes.

"She's your friend?" said Jack.

"Yes. We are old friends," said Tenzin. "*She* found *me* . . . I did not find her."

"Ohh . . . ," said Annie. "I understand now."

"What?" said Jack.

Annie smiled at him. "The snow leopard! *She's the Gray Ghost.*"

8

THE GRAY GHOST

"Wait a minute," said Jack, stunned. "The Gray Ghost is a snow leopard? And she is your friend?"

"Yes," said Tenzin. "In my youth, snow leopards were called Gray Ghosts. We thought of them as Guardians of the Mountains."

The snow leopard brushed her head gently against Tenzin's face. She kept her long furry tail wrapped around him.

"She's guarding you now, I think," said Annie.

"Yes, she is," said Tenzin quietly. "I told her of my sorrow."

"That's amazing," said Annie. "When did you first meet her?"

"Many years ago. Whenever I climbed alone, she would appear," Tenzin said. "Finally we sat together and looked at the world below. But I have not seen her since—" He looked away. "Since I lost my family."

The snow leopard still didn't move. As she stared at Jack and Annie, Jack remembered their rhyme:

The Gray Ghost of the Mountains,
The phantom of snow,
Has a secret to tell you
That very few know.

Alone on the hillside,
She hides in plain sight.
Her wisdom speaks softly
In shadows and light.

Jack looked into the big cat's soft green eyes. He looked hard and tried to grasp her wisdom.

The snow leopard held his gaze. Jack could tell that she was strong and gentle. But he couldn't figure out her secret.

Again, the cat brushed her head against Tenzin's face. Then she rose up and leapt from the rock.

The snow leopard seemed to fly through the air. She bounded up the slope until she was out of sight.

"Good-bye!" Annie called after her.

"Wait," said Tenzin. "In a moment, she will tell us good-bye herself."

"You mean she'll come back to us?" asked Annie.

"No. Look up, my friends." He pointed to a higher part of the mountain.

The snow leopard was perched on a rock. Her

fur blended into the gray of the mountain and the low clouds. She looked down at them.

Jack was astonished. *How did she get up there so fast?* he wondered. It was almost as if she'd vanished and then magically reappeared.

Tenzin laughed. "She always likes to be seen one last time," he said.

"I salute her," said Annie, bowing her head.

"Me too," whispered Jack.

Then the snow leopard was gone. When they

looked up, she'd vanished as quickly as she'd appeared.

Annie turned to Tenzin. "Thank you for helping us find the Gray Ghost," she said.

"Thank you for showing me the letter from your friend Morgan," said Tenzin. He jumped to his feet and stretched out his arms. He looked younger and stronger now.

"The day is going very well!" he said proudly. "Let us go back down and join the others!"

Tenzin started hiking back down the slope. Jack and Annie followed him.

Following Tenzin was much easier now than before. Heading down the slope, Jack and Annie stayed close behind him. If he got too far ahead, he waited for them.

By the time they reached Tenzin's hut, the clouds had started to lift. The day had grown warmer.

"Let us go down into the village!" said Tenzin.

"Right," said Jack. He and Annie grabbed their red backpacks and pulled them on.

When they turned around, they saw that Tenzin had already started down the path toward the village.

"Tenzin, wait!" called Annie.

Tenzin didn't seem to hear her. He kept walking.

"Tenzin!" Jack shouted as they hurried to catch up with him.

Tenzin stopped just as they came within sight of the village. "Look down below!" he called excitedly.

"Oh, wow!" said Annie.

Everything looked different now. The mountain village was no longer gloomy at all!

9

THE FESTIVAL

Bonfires were burning in the brown pasture. Red flames leapt into the air.

More travelers had arrived. Hikers wore backpacks and carried walking sticks. Everyone was watching villagers beat drums and dance around the fires. Many dancers wore bright red and purple clothing.

"The festival has begun!" said Tenzin.

"What *is* the festival?" said Jack.

"The Festival of Colors!" said Tenzin.

As they drew closer, Jack saw that the people at the festival all had brightly colored faces.

"Look at them!" Annie cried.

Everyone's face was painted with many colors: Rose red! Lime green! Sky blue! Lemon yellow!

"Tenzin! Jack! Annie!" Mina, Fuli, and Ama were shouting and running toward them.

Their faces were painted like everyone else's.

Ama showered blue powder over Jack, Annie, and Tenzin. Mina flung red and purple powders! Fuli tossed yellow and orange!

Soon all their faces and clothes were covered with bright colors! Everyone was laughing. They seemed happy, especially Tenzin.

"Your faces are rainbows!" he said to Jack and Annie.

"Yours too!" Annie said.

"We're so glad to see you!" said Mina. "Ama was worried!"

"Where were you, Tenzin?" Ama asked him.

"We went by your house and you weren't there. We couldn't find Jack and Annie, either!"

"I took them on a hike," said Tenzin. "You do not have to worry about me anymore, Ama. I am ready to live my life again."

Ama grinned. Her eyes were shining. "That is the best news I have ever heard," she said.

"Tenzin, join us!" said Fuli. She grabbed one of his hands. Mina grabbed the other. They pulled him toward the crowd.

"Come, Jack and Annie!" Fuli called over her shoulder.

As Jack and Annie headed into the pasture, Ama walked with them. "What has happened to Tenzin?" she said. "What did you do to help him?"

"We didn't do anything," said Jack.

"We just followed him up a high hill," said Annie.

"He's a great guide," said Jack. "Sometimes it was hard to keep up."

71

"That's all you did?" said Ama.

Jack and Annie glanced at each other. Jack shook his head. He didn't want to share their story of the Gray Ghost. That story belonged to Tenzin.

Annie seemed to understand. "Yes, that was pretty much it," she said to Ama.

"We just followed him," said Jack. He shrugged, as if the change in Tenzin was a mystery to him, too.

Ama laughed. "Well, whatever you did, he seems very joyful. Now maybe he will return to his old life."

"I'm sure he will!" said Jack. In that moment, he felt joyful, too. He was grateful that he and Annie had come to the Nepalese village.

"Have your parents arrived for the festival yet?" asked Ama. "Do you see them?"

Jack and Annie pretended to look for their mom and dad in the field full of dancers and people with painted faces.

Jack wished his parents *were* at the Festival of Colors. He imagined they'd be laughing and enjoying every minute. His parents loved holidays and celebrations—Christmas, Easter, the Fourth of July, Thanksgiving.

Annie seemed to feel the same thing. She turned to Ama. "Actually, they said we should meet them at noon by the stream. We were planning to all hike together today. They don't know about the festival."

Ama laughed. "When you find them, they will be surprised to see your painted faces. I hope you will bring them here. But if not, have a wonderful hike. The sun should come out soon."

"Thanks for taking care of us!" said Jack.

"Everyone, say good-bye to Jack and Annie," Ama called to the girls and Tenzin. "They have to go meet their parents!"

"Oh, no!" said Fuli. She and Mina ran over to Jack and Annie and hugged them.

Tenzin gave them a wide grin. Then he put his hands together and bowed his head.

Jack and Annie bowed to him, too. Then they bowed to Ama and her daughters.

"Thank you for everything," Jack said.

"We miss you already!" said Annie. She blew kisses to all of them, and Mina and Fuli blew kisses back.

Then Annie and Jack took off down the dirt path and left the pasture. They passed by the mountain stream and headed back into the hemlock grove.

Jack quickly found the rope ladder and started up. Annie followed, and they climbed into the magic tree house.

THE BEAUTY OF RAIN

Jack and Annie went to the window and looked down at the festival.

"There's Ama, Fuli, and Mina!" said Annie. "I see them dancing!"

"And look! Tenzin's dancing with them!" said Jack.

They both laughed.

"Wow!" said Annie. "Tenzin is a great dancer!"

"Hold on—" said Jack. He reached into his backpack and pulled out their guide book. He looked in the index for *Festival of Colors*. He read:

Nepal has more than fifty festivals each year. One of the best known is the Hindu festival of Holi. It is sometimes called the Festival of Colors because people throw colored powders and water on each other.

"Holi!" said Jack. He kept reading aloud:

Holi marks the end of winter and the coming of spring. Everyone celebrates beauty, the love of friends and family, and new beginnings.

"That's perfect!" said Annie. "Tenzin has a new beginning."

"Yes," said Jack. "Let's go home now and see Mom and Dad." He grabbed the Pennsylvania book and pointed at the picture of Frog Creek. "I wish we could go there!"

He and Annie waited for the wind to start

blowing. They waited for the tree house to start spinning.

But nothing happened.

"What's wrong?" said Jack.

"I don't know," said Annie. She pulled out their rhyme and read it again.

"Oh, no!" she said. "We didn't find out the *secret* of the snow leopard! We didn't write it down for Morgan!"

"Oh, man, I don't believe it," said Jack. "Maybe Tenzin can tell us her secret! We have to go back."

"Is he still dancing?" said Annie. They looked out the window.

"Yes, he is!" said Jack. "Let's go back down. We have to ask him!"

"Wait, wait!" said Annie. "Look! Look up there, Jack! See her on that cliff?"

"See who?" Jack asked.

"The Gray Ghost!" Annie whispered.

Jack looked up at the cliff and gasped.

The snow leopard was sitting alone, watching the festival of Holi from higher ground. Again, she was hiding in plain sight.

"I see her," Jack said softly.

In that moment, the leopard *did* seem to be the Guardian of the Mountains. The guardian of stone and fire and winter and spring. The guardian of

Tenzin, Mina, Fuli, Ama, and the whole village—
and travelers, too, like Annie and himself.

The sun broke through the clouds. For a
moment, dazzling light shone on the snow leopard.

The leopard's radiance lit a spark in Jack.

And, in that moment, he understood her secret.

"I've got it," he whispered. "Her secret."

"Quick, write it down!" said Annie.

Jack pulled out his notebook. He scribbled
down some words.

"I don't see her anymore," said Annie. "Do
you?"

Jack looked up again. The snow leopard had
vanished. "No," he said. "But I think I got her
secret. It came to me while I was looking at her.
Want to hear it?"

"Yes! But first, let's see if the tree house takes
us home now!" said Annie.

Jack picked up the Pennsylvania book again.
He pointed at the picture of Frog Creek.

"I wish we could go there!" he said. "HOME!"

Jack held his breath.

Then the wind started to blow.

"Yes!" said Jack.

"You *did* get it!" said Annie.

The tree house started to spin.

It spun faster and faster.

Then everything was still.

Absolutely still.

★ ★ ★

Rain was still falling in the Frog Creek woods.

Jack and Annie were wearing their yellow raincoats and rubber boots again. Their red backpacks had disappeared.

"Your face is clean," said Annie.

"Yours too," said Jack. "No more rainbow."

"So, what did you write down for Morgan?" asked Annie.

Jack reached into the pocket of his raincoat. His notebook was there. He pulled it out and looked at what he'd written.

"It sounds really simple now," Jack said, frowning.

"Read it to me," said Annie.

Jack read aloud:

Love hides in plain sight. We are never all alone.

"Whoa," said Annie. "It might sound simple. But it's deep."

"It is?" said Jack.

"Yes, Tenzin proved it," said Annie.

"How?" said Jack.

"After he lost his family, he felt all alone and just stayed in his house," said Annie. "But Morgan's note made him climb the mountain again. He found his old friend, the snow leopard. The Guardian of the Mountains. And she reminded him that she was always there, that love is all around us, protecting us. Even when we can't see it."

Jack nodded thoughtfully. "Okay . . . ," he said.

"And remember him dancing at the festival, so happy to be surrounded by people who love him?" said Annie. "Well, their love was always there, too, even when he was staying alone in his house. He just forgot it for a while."

"Right," said Jack. "That *is* deep."

He tore the page out of his notebook and left it on the floor for Morgan.

"Let's go home to Mom and Dad now," said Annie, and she started down the rope ladder.

Jack followed. As he and Annie walked through the woods, their boots squished over the soggy ground.

"The rain is so beautiful," said Annie.

"Yes," said Jack. To his surprise, it really was. The wet wintry trees were beautiful, too, every bare gray branch, every dead brown leaf.

83

The rain would help bring life back soon and make everything green again.

Jack and Annie came out of the Frog Creek woods and started down the sidewalk toward their house.

"I wish we could tell Mom and Dad about our trip," said Annie.

"Right. Picture that," said Jack. "Hi, Mom and Dad! Annie and I took a walk and went all the way to Nepal. We made friends with Mina, Fuli, Ama, Tenzin—"

"And a snow leopard called the Gray Ghost!" said Annie. "She's the Guardian of the Mountains!"

"We slept in a tea house in sleeping bags," said Jack, "and we ate lentil stew that tasted just like yours, Mom."

Annie laughed. "And we went to a spring festival, where people tossed colored powders on each other," she said. "And us!"

"Mom and Dad, you would have loved that festival," said Jack. "And hiking with us, too."

"Yeah, and you would have loved our friends, especially the snow leopard!" said Annie. "We wished you were with us!"

"We did. We *really* did," said Jack.

Without another word, the two of them took off running down the sidewalk. They ran through the beautiful rain, heading for home.

Turn the page for a sneak peek at

Magic Tree House® Fact Tracker

Snow Leopards and Other Wild Cats

MAGIC TREE HOUSE®

FACT TRACKER

Snow Leopards
and Other Wild Cats

A NONFICTION COMPANION TO
MAGIC TREE HOUSE #36:
Sunlight on the
Snow Leopard

Mary Pope Osborne and Jenny Laird

Today's Pets

These days, cats are the most popular pets in the world! Dogs may be man's best friend, but across the globe, people have more cats in their homes than any other animal.

Although the cats that share our homes are domesticated, at times, they do some wild things. Have you ever wondered why cats scratch at furniture? Or attack a ball of yarn?

These actions are a lot like the survival behaviors of wild cats. Our pet cats come from fierce ancestors. So, even though they no longer need to hunt for their meals, they haven't lost their wild cat instincts.

Cats have scent glands in their paws. Wild cats scratch trees to mark their territory with their smell and with claw marks.

The bark also keeps their claws clean and sharp.

Things that move or dangle look like food or danger to cats. In the wild, cats compete with snakes for food, so anything shaped like a snake wakes up their fighting instincts!

Wild Cats

Today there are about thirty-six different *species*, or kinds, of wild cats in the world.

A species is a group of plants or animals that are alike in certain ways.

They live on every continent except Australia and Antarctica.

Most cat species thrive where there are plenty of trees. But some do well in open prairies, *savannas*, or even deserts. Many live where it's warm, but others survive well in cold weather.

Some species can live in many kinds of *habitats*. You might picture tigers in a rain forest, but they also live in mountains that are rocky.

A <u>savanna</u> is a grassy plain with few trees.

A <u>habitat</u> is a place where certain animals live, which has the climate, food, water, and plants they need to survive.

Big and Small Cats

Wild cats come in all different sizes: small, medium, and huge! But they are often divided into just two groups: big cats and small cats. Or sometimes, roaring cats and purring cats.

Why? Because there are only four kinds of cats that can roar, and they are also the largest felines in the cat family. So most scientists use the term *big cats* to refer to the cats that can roar—tigers, lions, jaguars, and leopards—and *small cats* to refer to the cats that can purr but cannot roar.

Only cats and their near relatives can purr. Big cats can roar because they have a special U-shaped bone in their throats.

Snow leopards are an unusual case. They make a purrlike noise, but it doesn't sound like the purring of small cats. And they can't roar. But, because they are very closely related to the cats that do roar, most scientists agree snow leopards belong in the big cat group.

Big Cats
Lions
Tigers
Jaguars
Leopards
Snow leopards

Sorting cats into groups can get tricky, but all cats, large and small, belong to one big family. Scientists call it the Felidae family.

The black-footed cat of Africa weighs about four pounds. The Siberian tiger weighs up to 700 pounds. Believe it or not, these cats are related!

Cloud Climbers

Snow leopards live higher up than any other cat. In the Himalayas, snow leopards have been found living 18,000 feet above sea level. That's almost four miles high! Most humans will only reach those kinds of heights in an airplane.

Living high up isn't easy for any creature. The climate is cold and dry. The *terrain* is rocky and steep. Food is hard to find. There is less oxygen at higher altitudes, making it harder to breathe. So how do snow leopards manage to survive in areas where no other big cat could? Because of *adaptation* (a-dap-TAY-shun). Over time, their bodies have changed, or *adapted*, to make them perfectly suited for their extreme environment.

Guinness World Records lists the snow leopard as the highest-living land predator.

Terrain is the physical features of a piece of land.

Little Big Cats

Snow leopards are the smallest of the big cats. They are about the height of a golden retriever and weigh between 60 and 120 pounds. Despite their name, snow leopards are more closely related to tigers than leopards. But tigers are the biggest cats in the world. They're a foot taller than snow leopards and weigh *hundreds* of pounds more!

Ghosts of the Mountains

The snow leopards' spooky ability to disappear into the rocks and snow has earned them the nickname *ghosts of the mountains*. These "ghosts" seem mysterious because so few people have ever seen one. But snow leopards probably avoid humans mostly because they are shy. If a person approaches them, they simply run away.

Unlike most other big cats, snow leopards don't often fight each other over land or food.

Snow leopards also try to avoid one another. Except when females are rearing their young cubs, snow leopards don't have dens or permanent homes. They are almost always on the move. They often have to travel great distances in search of food.

Keep Away
Snow leopards have three more ways of telling other cats that they're in the neighborhood and visitors are not welcome!

Scratching tree trunks
with their claws

To keep from bumping into another cat along the way, they leave special "keep away" messages. Like many animals, they will spray rocks and trees with urine to mark their territory.

This spot is taken!

Rubbing against rocks to leave their scent

Please do not disturb!

Scraping the ground with their hind legs

Magic Tree House®

Magic Tree House® Merlin Missions

Magic Tree House® Super Edition

#1: World at War, 1944

Magic Tree House® Fact Trackers

More Magic Tree House®